KU-825-630

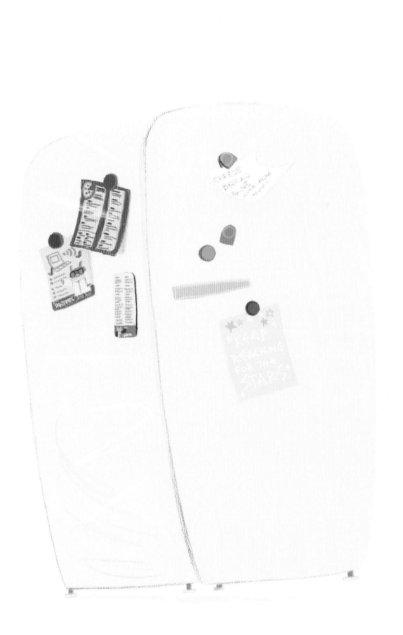

Oh, it's **you** again.
What an original thing to do,
open a book you were told not to.

Well, allow me to give you a round
of applause. **Congratulations!**
You've had your thrill.
You can now put the book down.

How did you get to this page?

We agreed you were putting
the book down.

Oh, I know what's
happened.

You got startled knowing you
were doing the wrong thing so
you dropped the book and it fell
to the ground open on this page.
No harm done.

Just **please** don't
turn again.

What on earth!
You turned **again!**

I'm hurt but not alarmed
'cause look over there.

That whole page is made
of lead. One of the heaviest
metals in the entire world.
Way too **heavy** for you
to lift, so don't even bother
trying to turn the page.

100%
REALLY HEAVY
LEAD

Okay, I lied about the lead. It was just paint.
So, don't go thinking you're strong or anything.

But I'm definitely not lying when I tell you
that the next page is

really, really

HOT.

Hotter than the sun,

so DON'T touch it!!

You'll BURN yourself.

Definitely DON'T

turn the page.

After the last book,
I did a deal with a goblin
to transform me back to
my regular age, but he had
one condition: that no one
read this book.

The Art of the GOBLIN Deal

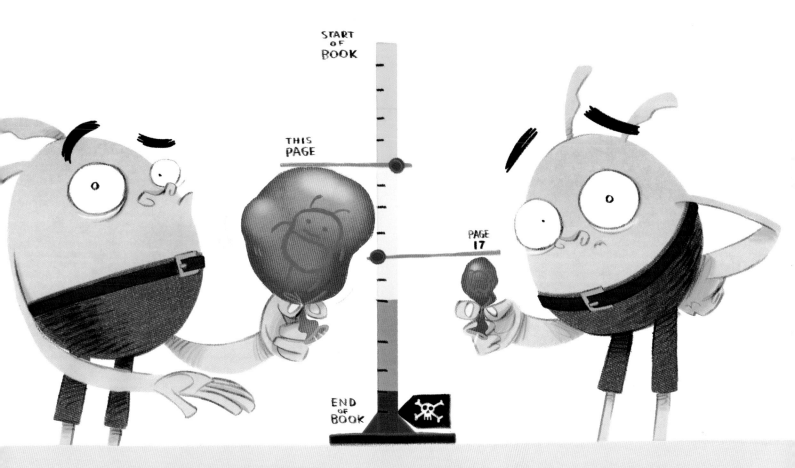

START
OF
BOOK

THIS
PAGE

PAGE
17

END
OF
BOOK

If someone does, his spell kicks in! Have you not noticed?
With every page you turn I'm **shrinking** in size!
Turn one more page and I'll prove it.

That's my FRIDGE!!!

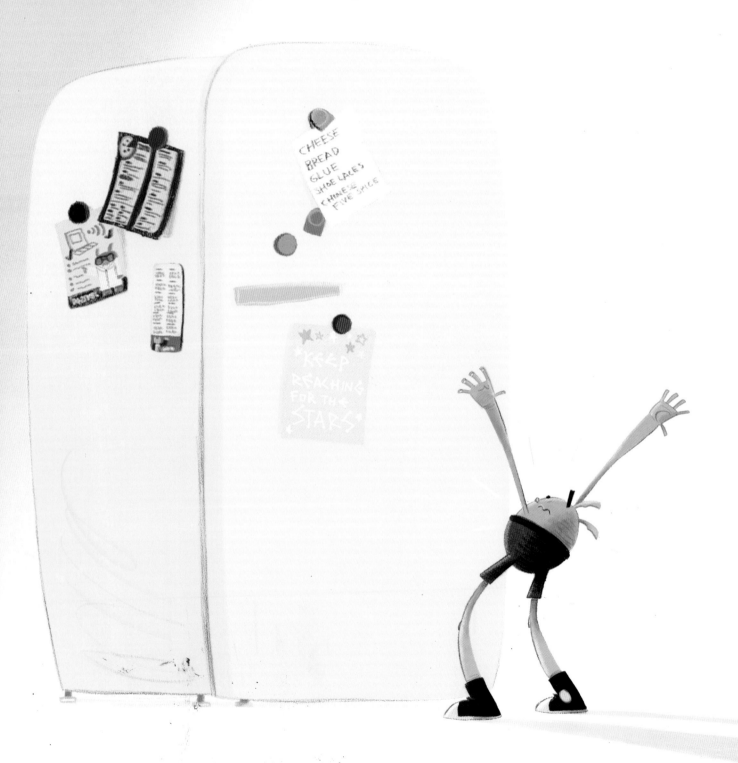

Look, I can barely reach the handle. If you keep turning the page, I won't be able to get myself any food and I'll perish.

YOU MUST STOP RIGHT NOW!

Please **don't turn the page.**

AhhHH!

You turned AGAIN!!!

Oh, wow, look how **big** the chocolate is!

This is actually wonderful. When Mum says I'm only allowed two squares of chocolate, I usually complain, but this would last me a month.

Woo hoo!
I like being this size, so PLEASE don't turn the page.

Holy heck!

You're NOT stopping, but the chocolate is even bigger now so that's a plus.

What about clothes though?

All of my other clothes are now waaaay too big and I can't wear what I've got on forever.

PLEASE TURN BACK, I can't bear the thought of wearing the same undies for the rest of my life.

Geepus!

I'm smaller again, which means I'm in these undies for eternity.

They are going to **stink** to high heaven.

Hang on, I know!

I can borrow some clothes off my teddies.

Yep, these **fit nicely**.

So, can we agree that you leave me on this page with the **HUGE** chocolate and my lovely new clothes that fit?

Oh my word,

YOU'VE TURNED AGAIN
and now my new clothes
are also too big!

Thump, thump.

What's that sound?

Thump!

HOLY CRUMPETS.

I can see what's coming and I normally wouldn't be scared but now that I'm small it's TERRIFYING.

TURN BACK,
TURN BACK!

JUST DON'T TURN THE PAGE!!

AHHHHHH!!!

An ant!
A giant ant.
It's a gi-ANT!!

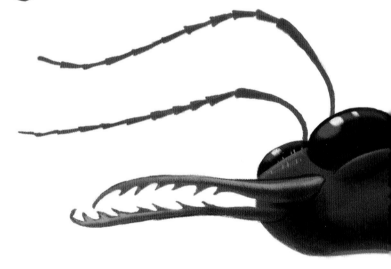

This is how cavemen must have felt with all those prehistoric creatures coming at them.

Easy, girl... easy! Settle down. Quick, get me off this page!

Oh! The ant is quite kind. It turns out she was just as **scared** of me as I was of her. She didn't mean any harm. I should remember that if I ever get big again.

Look, this is NOT my preferred situation but now I have an ant that can take me places and the smallest speck of food could feed me for a week so I'm **happy** enough here.

Please, don't turn the page.

Okay... my tricks haven't worked, my pleas have been ignored, and my Gi-ant ran away when she saw me halve in size again, so you've left me no choice. Here comes a THREAT!

You can turn the page if you like,
but I'll be so small that you won't be able to see me.

And mark my words,

I'm going to
JUMP onto you.

I'm going to
LIVE on you.

Perhaps CRAWL into your nose and **tickle** your nose hairs.

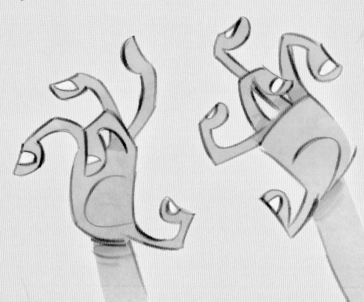

So, **DO NOT** turn the page...
or else!!!!

THAT'S IT!
I'm coming for you!

Although being this tiny means
it's going to take me some
time to get there so...

DO
NOT
CLOSE
THE
BOOK!